D1364775

HOLIDAYS & CELEBRATIONS

Carron Brown

Illustrated by Ipek Konak

Kane Miller
A DIVISION OF EDC PUBLISHING

Festivals and special days
happen at certain times of the
year all over the world.

People get together with friends
and family to celebrate.

Shine a flashlight behind the page
or hold it to the light to reveal
the hidden delights of each holiday.
Discover a world of great surprises.

This park in China has been decorated with red lanterns for Lunar New Year.

What's on the end of these sticks?

It's a dragon! Its long body is moved up and down.

In many Asian communities, Lunar New Year marks the start of spring. The "dragon dance" is thought to bring good luck for the year.

It's February 14.

What's inside
this envelope?

A Valentine's Day card!

People all over the world
celebrate this day by sending
cards to their loved ones.
Sometimes the cards are left
unsigned, for a fun surprise!

In India, these children are throwing colorful powdered paint at each other.

What else adds to the fun?

Squirt!

Water! The water makes
the paint powder stick.

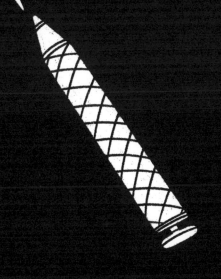

The children are celebrating
Holi, the Hindu festival of colors.
People dance, sing, and have a lot of fun.

On Saint Patrick's Day, in Chicago,
Illinois, the Chicago River
is turned green with
a special dye.

What's coming out from
under the bridge?

A boat full of people!

This day is all about celebrating Irish culture. People wear green clothes, and the river is dyed green because of Ireland's many lush, green hills and fields.

It's the first night of Passover, a Jewish holiday. This family has gathered for the Seder.

What's under the napkin?

A piece of matzo!

Matzo is a special unleavened bread
eaten during Passover, and a piece
has been broken off and saved for
later—it's called the afikoman.

It will be the last
food eaten during the
Passover Seder.

It's Hanami, the cherry
blossom festival,
in Japan.

Who's sitting
beneath the
trees?

It's a family having a picnic.

In Spring, the cherry trees are full of beautiful blossoms, and people gather beneath them.

In the garden, children are searching high and low.

What are they looking for?

Easter eggs!

Easter is a Christian holiday
that takes place each spring.

Easter-egg hunts are a popular tradition
to celebrate the day. (Sometimes the
eggs are made of chocolate!)

Everyone's dressed in their best clothes for Eid.

What's behind the balloons?

Yum—lots of food!

This Muslim festival is a time
for giving, saying thanks,
and eating together.

It's the Fourth of July, Independence Day. The Sound of a marching band fills the air.

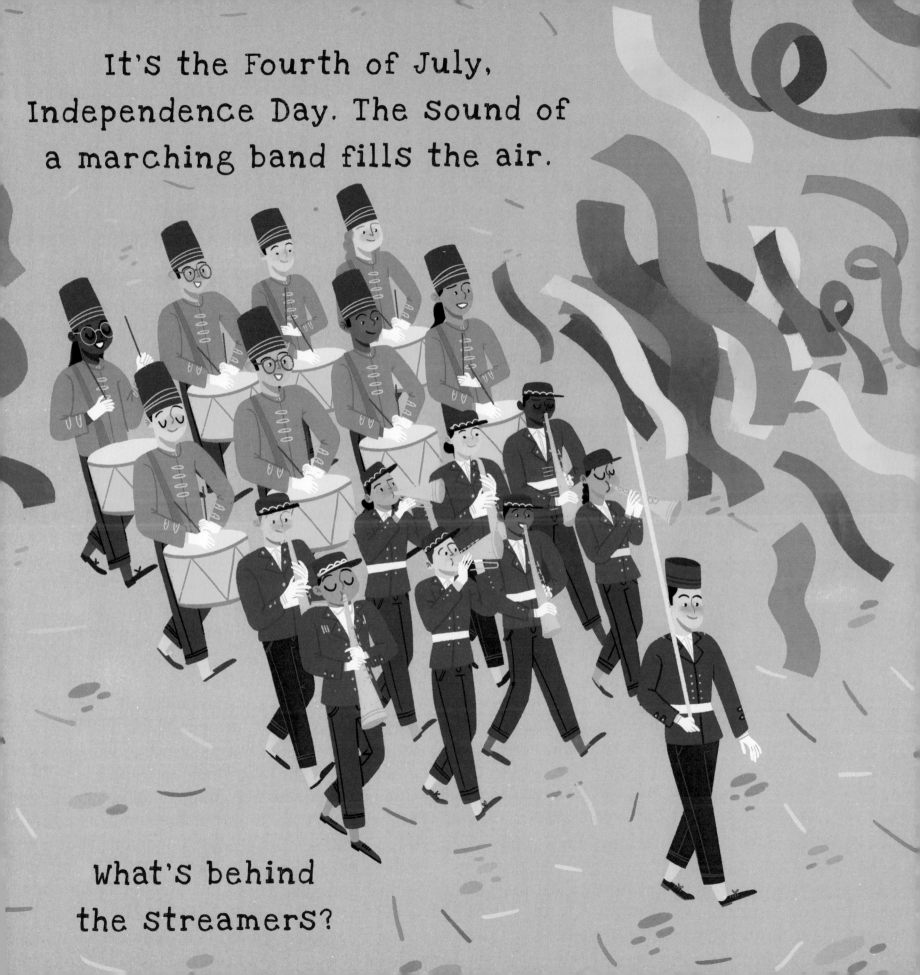

What's behind the streamers?

The American flag!

The person who carries it is
called the standard-bearer.

Independence Day celebrates
the day the United States became
a country: July 4, 1776.

A tomato!

At the La Tomatina festival in Spain, people throw tomatoes at each other—just for fun!

October 31 is Halloween!
It is a day for costumes
and treats.

What's
beneath
this
sheet?

Boo!

A girl—she's wearing
a ghost costume.

Kids around the world dress up
in Halloween costumes (some are
spooky!) to go trick-or-treating.

It's the Day of the
Dead in Mexico.

People are placing food
and gifts on the ofrenda
(altar). What else is
on the ofrenda?

There are pictures
of family members.

It's a time to remember
happy things about people
who have died.

It's the last night of Hanukkah, and all nine candles on the menorah, the special candle holder, are lit.

What are these children watching?

A dreidel! This spinning top is part
of a game. Children play to win
chocolate coins or other items.

This eight-day Jewish holiday
is a time for families to gather,
give gifts, and play games.

The Christmas tree is shining with beautiful lights and ornaments.

What are the children excited about?

Presents!

Christmas is a wintertime Christian festival.
On Christmas Day, people celebrate in lots
of different ways, including giving gifts.

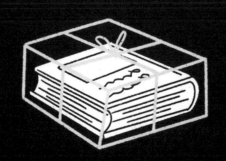

Red, green, and black decorations are put up for Kwanzaa. It is a time for celebrating African American culture.

What is this family doing?

Lighting a candle! Each
candle stands for one of the
seven principles of Kwanzaa.

The colors have meanings too:
black for the people, red for
past struggles, and green
for future hopes.

At midnight on January 1, there's a cheering crowd and fireworks. A whole year of celebrations is about to start again.

Happy New Year!

There's more...

Lunar New Year
This spring festival marks the end of winter and the start of a new year in many Asian communities. It happens in January or February.

Valentine's Day
February 14 is a day for people to show their love. People send cards to each other and sometimes give gifts, too.

Holi
This colorful Hindu festival celebrates love and the beginning of spring. It usually takes place in March.

St. Patrick's Day
March 17 celebrates the life of Saint Patrick of Ireland. People wear green and watch parades of bands and Irish dancers.

Passover
This Jewish holiday lasts for seven to eight days, starting on the 15th day of the Hebrew month of Nisan. Families tell stories, sing, and eat together.

Cherry Blossom Festival
This ancient tradition encourages people to appreciate nature. Families and friends in Japan visit parks and gardens to walk and picnic by the flowering cherry trees.

Easter
This is an important Christian holiday that takes place in spring. Eggs at Easter are a symbol of new life and new beginnings.

Eid

An important Muslim festival, Eid is the end of Ramadan—a month when adults fast during the day. It happens on the first day of the Islamic month of Shawwāl.

Day of the Dead

This Mexican festival happens from October 31 to November 2. There are parades, and people remember their loved ones by decorating ofrendas with flowers—especially marigolds—and lighting candles.

The Fourth of July

Independence Day is celebrated in the US every July 4. People wear the colors of the American flag—red, white, and blue.

Hanukkah

The Jewish festival of lights starts on the 25th day of the Hebrew month Kislev, and lasts for eight days. A candle on the menorah is lit for every night of Hanukkah.

La Tomatina Festival

This takes place every year in the town of Buñol, Spain, on the last Wednesday of August. When it's done, the tomato mush is cleared from the streets by hoses.

Christmas

This Christian festival celebrates the birth of Jesus Christ. It always takes place on December 25.

Halloween

Halloween originally began as a religious celebration in Ireland and Scotland. Now, it is celebrated across the world.

Kwanzaa

From December 26 to January 1, this US festival celebrates traditional African food, music, and storytelling. Gifts are given on the last day.